Happiness
is a
Watermelon
on Your Head

To my friends Anja, Karin, Babs and their families. S.D.

To Alice and Jesse. Wishing you lives filled with watermelons and much other silliness. D.H.

Happiness is a Watermelon on Your Head

ISBN: 978-1-907912-05-4

First published in Portuguese in 2011 under the title *A Felicidade é uma Melancia na Cabeça* by Callis Editora, São Paulo, Brazil
This edition published in Great Britain by Phoenix Yard Books, 2012

Phoenix Yard Books Ltd
Phoenix Yard
65 King's Cross Road
London
WC1X 9LW
www.phoenixyardbooks.com

Copyright © Stella Dreis, 2010
English text copyright © Daniel Hahn, 2012

1 3 5 7 9 10 8 6 4 2

A CIP catalogue record for this book is available from the British Library

Printed in Singapore

Happiness is a Watermelon on Your Head

Stella Dreis

Text by Daniel Hahn

At the end of the village, behind a green door,
Lived happy Miss Jolly, with Melvin, her boar.
Each morning she'd sit in her tree playing a song
On her cello, while Melvin sang sweetly along.

"What makes her so happy? We really must learn!"
Cried her neighbours, Miss Whimper, Miss Grouch and Miss Stern.
"It's *awful* being miserable day after day.
Let's find out her secret! There must be a way!"

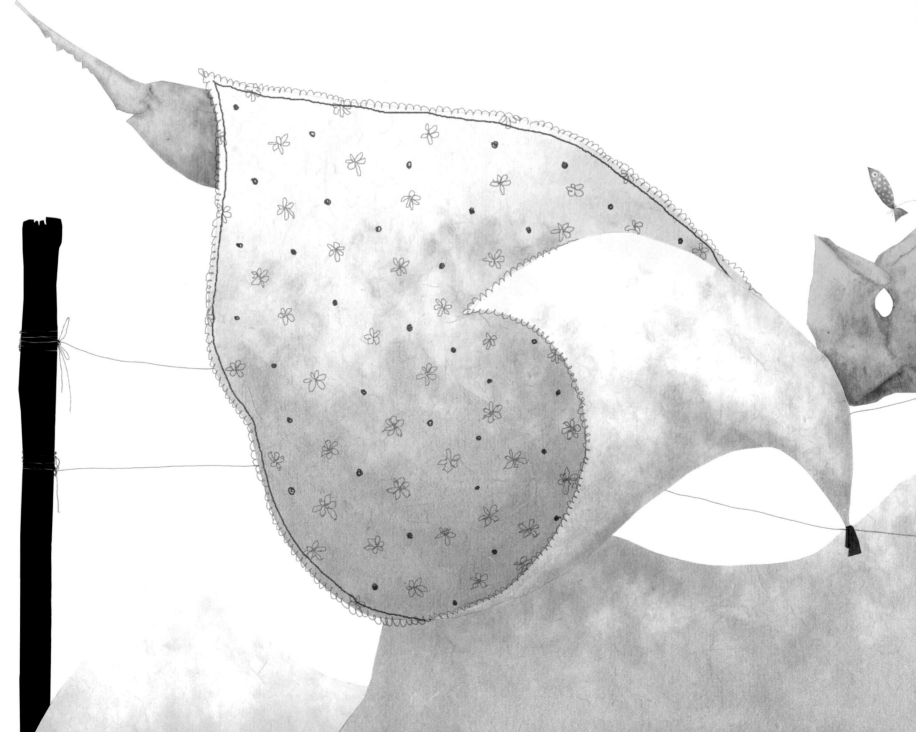

The very next day, what a sight met their eye!
It's happy Miss Jolly, just frolicking by,

With a smile on her face, and
"**Good morning!**" she said,
With a skip in her step . . .

"That's it!" cried Miss Stern, "that's the trick! It's so clever!
We need hats made of food! We'll be happy forever!"

So they ran to her kitchen and rummaged about
For a nice bunch of radishes, cauliflower, trout . . .

Then they strapped them all on,
tied them fast, pinned them down,
And stepped out –
delighted –
to dazzle the town.

Such beautiful hats!
What a sight! What a show!

Did those hats make them happy now?

. . . No.

So . . .

They tried clocks, they tried pots,
they tried forks,
they tried twigs,
Fantastical whatsits and thingamajigs.

Their hats were ingenious, remarkable, mad!

But how were the women?
Still *dreadfully* sad.

Nothing worked.
"Try the cello!" said one, "Climb the tree!
Maybe *that's* why Miss Jolly's more happy than me."

"That's it!" cried her friends and began their ascent,
Higher and higher and higher they went . . .

But like four large, ripe fruits, so heavy and round,
They all – with the cello – *thumped* back to the ground.

"But wait," cried Miss Grouch,
"I've the best idea yet!"

"Maybe being happy is *having a pet!*
Miss Jolly has Melvin, you know. *What a boar!*"

"We'll have birds!" said Miss Whimper,
"and monkeys galore!"

"Something green!"
said Miss Stern.
"**Something long!** Something small!"

And they did. And what happened then?

Nothing at all.

So that's it.
They gave up.
What else could they do?
They were sadder than ever.
(Their pets were sad, too.)

As they dragged themselves homeward, in gloom and despair,
A giant green *something* came flying through the air –
It brushed past the tip of a rocking-horse hat
As it whizzed through the air and came down with a ...

SPLAT!

A watermelon!

"*Attaaaaaaack!*" cried Miss J, and she showered them with fruit
As she raced through the town (with her boar in pursuit).
Soon the battle had spread to stupendous excess,
And the whole of the town was a pink, sticky mess.

When the chaos was done, as they lay on the ground,
Miss Whimper, Miss Stern and Miss Grouch looked around.
They were covered with pips and with pulp and with goo,
One had juice in her hat, one had seeds in her shoe,

They lay there, defeated, exhausted and sore,
Those three sorry women (and Melvin, the boar),
Then one of the women . . .

But wait – what's this?
Could that be the trace
Of a smirk, or a grin, or a . . .
smile on her face?

Yes!

All sticky and slimy and pink – what a sight!
They giggled and hooted and danced with delight.

"We did it! We did it!" Their sadness had passed.
And they laughed, and they laughed, and were happy at last.

Stella Dreis

Stella Dreis was born in 1972 in Plovdiv, Bulgaria.
In 1995 she received a scholarship for gifted students
to the Academy of Fashion Design in Hamburg. After completing her degree,
Stella spent several years working and travelling in the fashion industry. In 2002 she returned
to drawing and illustrating. Several projects and exhibitions were followed by her first children's
picture book in 2008, *The City that Went Off.* Stella's take on the Hans Christian Andersen classic,
The Princess and the Pea, 2009, was voted one of the seven best children's books of the year in Germany.

Daniel Hahn

Daniel Hahn is a writer, editor and translator. He has translated fiction by novelists including
José Eduardo Agualusa, José Luís Peixoto and María Dueñas (winning the Independent Foreign Fiction
Prize with Agualusa's *The Book of Chameleons*); and non-fiction by writers ranging from Portuguese
Nobel laureate José Saramago to Brazilian footballer Pelé. He is also one of the editors of the
Ultimate Book Guides, an award-winning series of reading guides for children and teenagers,
and is currently assembling a new *Oxford Companion to Children's Literature.*
This is his first picture book.